Grief is Like a Snowflake

Activity and Idea Book

published by

National Center for Youth Issues

Practical Guidance Resources
Educators Can Trust

ncyi.org

A special "**Thanks!**" to **Cathy Fox** –
One of the best program directors in the business!

Note to Grief Facilitators, Educators, and Parents:

Grief is like a snowflake. Every person experiences grief in their own unique way. Like snow, sometimes grief comes one flake at a time, other times it comes like a blizzard. It melts away, but it always comes back.

The book is designed to offer grief facilitators, educators, and parents "hands on" activities that explore grief. Participants will gain a better understanding of what grief is, how to personalize it, and how to endure the grieving process. I hope these activities will be helpful to many who are going through difficult transitions.

I would personally like to thank the Ted E. Bear Hollow team for helping me make this project possible.

Thoughtfully,
Julia Cook

Ted E. Bear Hollow
Mending the hearts of grieving children and teens

www.tedebearhollow.org

Duplication and Copyright

National Center for Youth Issues
Practical Guidance Resources
Educators Can Trust
ncyi.org

P.O. Box 22185
Chattanooga, TN 37422-2185
423.899.5714 • 800.477.8277
fax: 423.899.4547
www.ncyi.org

ISBN: 978-1-931636-35-3
© 2011 National Center for Youth Issues, Chattanooga, TN
All rights reserved.

Summary: A supplementary teacher's guide for *Grief is Like a Snowflake.*
Full of discussion questions and exercises to share with students.

Written by: Julia Cook
Illustrations by: Anita DuFalla
Published by National Center for Youth Issues

Printed at Starkey Printing
Chattanooga, TN, USA
September 2011

A "Hole" New ME!

Objective: To recognize changes that occur after someone dies. We adjust to these changes over time and create a "new normal," but our grief will always be with us.

Materials Needed:
One figure per group member
Crayons and markers
Paper punch
Small heart-shaped stickers

•

At the beginning of the first session, allow each group member to decorate a figure to represent themselves.

•

After decorating, have group members punch one hole in their cut outs for each session they will have (i.e. punch 8 holes for 8 sessions etc.) Make sure the holes are not too close together.

• After the holes are punched, talk about how we are changed after someone dies, much like the holes have permanently changed the figures. Yet, with the support and love of others, we learn how to cope with our grief.

• At the end of every session, allow group members to place one heart sticker over a hole in their figures. Have each person share one thing from that session that will help on his or her grief journey.

• At the end of the final session, each hole should be patched with a sticker. If desired, a photo can be taken at each stage – after decorating, after punching the holes, and after covering the final hole – to demonstrate the growth the person has accomplished throughout the sessions.

Ice Cream Sundae Celebration

Materials Needed:
- One bowl per group member
- 1 scoop of vanilla ice cream per group member
- Chocolate sauce
- Nuts
- 1 can of whipped topping
- Cherries
- Spoons
- Smiles

Objective: To spend time together as a group in sharing memories and celebrating the lives of those who died.

Have each group member place 1 scoop of vanilla ice cream into the bowl and respond to the associated memory question below. Repeat this step for the other ingredients until each person has taken turns with all ingredients and shared 5 memories.

(Allow group members to pass if they want to.)

Ice Cream: What was the person's favorite food?

Chocolate Sauce: Share a holiday or birthday memory.

Nuts: Share something funny that the person said or did.

Whipped Topping: What was something the person was great at doing?

Cherry: What was your favorite thing to do with that person?

Have each person grab a spoon. Enjoy as a group and celebrate all of their positive memories with a sweet treat.

My Lifesavers!

Objective: To identify the lifesavers in your life!

Materials Needed:
- 1 roll of white or colored Life Savers candy per child, or several large individually wrapped Life Savers candies per child.
- 1 fine point permanent marker
- Paper and pencil
- Yarn or string

A life saver is a person, activity or thing that helps you through life and brings you support. Lifesavers help you through tough times as well as happy times and are always there for you when you need them most. Make a list of the lifesavers in your life.

Carefully write the names of each of your "lifesavers" on the Life Savers candies with a fine point marker. Use one Life Saver per name. You can write on the flat side of the Life Saver or along the edge.

String the Life Savers onto the yarn and wear them around your neck as a necklace. This way, your Life Savers will always be close to you.

Extension:
Use colored craft foam to make lifesavers instead of actual candy Life Savers.

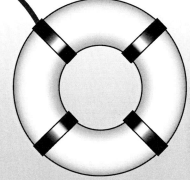

Another "My Lifesavers!" Activity

Objective: To identify the lifesavers in your life!

Have each person cut red construction paper into strips and using markers, write the names of their "lifesavers" – (people, activities, or things) on each strip. Glue each strip around the ring and add twine to create the nautical lifesaver ring.

Hang this up in your room so that you will always feel close to your lifesavers.

Materials Needed:
- One white Styrofoam ring per group member.
  (These can be found at craft stores or in floral departments.)
- Red construction paper
- Markers
- Glue
- Scissors
- Twine

Heavyweights

Objective: To identify the thoughts and emotions that weigh heavily on us and also identify strategies that can help us lift some of the weight.

Materials Needed:
- Backpack
- Books

Directions:

Have group members pair up. One person will be the griever and the other will be the helper. Instruct the grievers to put on an empty backpack. Have them list their heavy feelings and thoughts. For each one they list, the helper must place a book in their backpack.

After several minutes, instruct the grievers to then list ways in which they care for themselves (e.g. talking to a friend or family member, eating well, getting enough sleep). For each one they list, the helper will take out one book.

Switch roles and repeat the activity so everyone has a chance to be a griever and a helper.

After the activity, discuss as a group what this was like for them. What did it feel like to be a griever and have all of those feelings weighing heavily on them? What did it feel like to be a helper and have to put the weight on the griever? How did it feel to take the weight off? How helpful were the helpers: did they offer suggestions and assistance, or just do as they were told? Relate this to their grief experiences.

Pocket Notes

Objective: To provide group members an outlet for their feelings and offer an interactive support.

Directions:

Use a pocket from an old pair of pants or create one using paper. Hang the pocket somewhere easily accessible in the room.

In the first group session, let group members know that this pocket is for them to use. They can write anonymous notes and place them in the pocket and can read and respond to notes in there. They may have a question to ask or some feelings to express. With the pocket notes, they can do so anonymously. Group members can then read notes that are in there and write a message back.

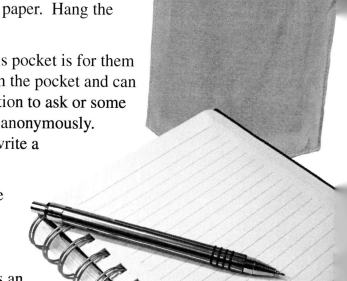

During the last session, encourage group members to write notes to future group members. They can reflect on how nervous they felt at the beginning and offer reassurance and support to new group members. Then, during the first session of the next group, members can read these notes as an icebreaker.

Grief is Like a Snowflake

Objective: To help children realize that grief is unique to each person. Just like no two snowflakes are alike, no two people will grieve the same. Also like a snowflake, sometimes grief comes one flake at a time… other times, it comes like a blizzard. It always melts, but it always comes back.

Directions:

1 Have each person fold their piece of paper in half forming a triangle. (figure A)

2 Have each person fold their triangle in half again. (figure B)

3 Have each person fold their triangle in half two more times (as shown)

4 Using the scissors, cut shapes into your folded triangle. You can cut any shapes that you would like and cut as many as you would like.

5 Unfold your snowflake and compare it to others in your group. Although they all started out the same, they all look different from one another – no two are alike.

6 Using the dental floss and paper clips, hang each snow flake from the ceiling in your room as a reminder that everyone grieves differently.

Materials Needed:
- One 9 inch by 9 inch square piece of paper per group member
- One pair of scissors per person (use safety scissors with younger children.)
- Dental floss and paper clips

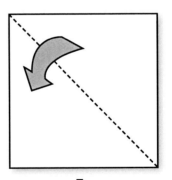

A

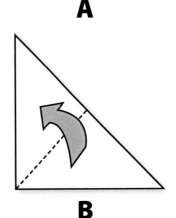

B

SOCK It To 'Em!

Objective: To help group members deal with the anger associated with the death of their special person.

Materials Needed:
- One tube sock for each group member
- One blank sheet of paper
- Markers (or colored pencils)

Directions:

- Pass out a sheet of paper and one tube sock to each member of the group.

- As a group, talk about how it is very normal to feel angry after someone dies. Give the group several minutes to silently write out or draw all of their angry and negative thoughts and feelings on both sides of the paper. (Use colored marker or pencils to represent feelings.) When they are done, have each person crumple and tear up their paper and put the pieces inside of his/her sock.

- Tie each sock in a knot so that the pieces of paper are trapped in the toe area of the socks.

- Talk about how sometimes it is hard to control angry feelings. When we are feeling this way, it is not ok to hurt ourselves or others with words or actions but it is ok to feel angry. We can let our anger out in safe and healthy ways.

- Allow each person to smack the wall with their anger socks. If possible, take the group outside and allow them to throw their socks to let out their anger.

- **Sock it to 'Em!** and let go of all of your negative feelings and thoughts! Let it out! Take it out on the wall!!!

Grief Survival Kit

Objective: Everyone needs a survival kit to get through the tough times:

Directions: Print off the sheet below and allow group members to assemble their own kits as you speak about each item and why it is needed. Use a lunch-sized paper bag as a container and have each group member decorate their bag in memory of the person who died.

Grief Survival Kit includes:

- **TOOTHPICK** – To help you pick out the good memories
- **PAPER CLIP** – To help you to hold it all together.
- **PENNY** – To remind you to keep a good "cents" of balance. Also to remind you that change can be good.
- **GEM STONE** – You are a unique gem! Shine brightly
- **RUBBER BAND** – To remind you of hugging…those times when you need to give a hug or when you want to receive one. Also, remember to be FLEXIBLE!
- **BAND-AID** – For healing both on the inside and on the outside.
- **TISSUE** – To remind you that it's ok to cry.
- **ERASER** – Everyone makes mistakes and that's OK!
- **LIFE SAVER** – It is OK to be one and to need one!!!
- **STICK (OR STICKER)** – To remind you to "Stick with it!" You will get through this!
- **HONEY PACKET** – "You get more bees with honey than you do vinegar!"
- **GUM DROP** – To remind you "Don't Be Afraid to Drop!"
- **BOUNCY BALL** – Because it's ok to have fun too! Sometimes you just need to bounce something!
- **PIPE CLEANER** – To help with all the twists and turns along your grief journey.
- **BALLOON** – To let out all of your hot air.
- **COTTON BALL/PUFF BALL** – A "warm fuzzy" to keep close
- **SAFETY PIN** – To keep your special memories close to you.
- **SMARTIES** – For all you have learned and all you will learn on your grief journey.

My Grief Survival Kit

A Mess of Feelings

Objective: To recognize the mix of feelings following a death and how difficult it can be to sort them out.

Materials Needed:
- Various colors of clay or Play-doh
- Ziploc bags

Directions:

- As a group, brainstorm a list of the many feelings they have experienced since their special person died.

- Instruct each member to think of four feelings they have experienced. Tell them to pick a different color to represent each of these feelings and make a ball of clay for each to represent the intensity of this feeling for them. For instance, if they have a lot of anger, they would make a large ball of clay. If they have a little sadness, they would make a little ball. Have the group members share what feelings they selected.

- After sharing, instruct group members to place all four balls in their bag and smash it up. When we are grieving, our feelings get all mixed up. Sometimes, we may see more of one than another, but it is hard to separate them.

Recipe for Feelings

Objective: Determine your own recipe to deal with your grief.

Materials Needed:
- Recipe cards or index cards
- Pencils

Directions: Brainstorm as a group a list of negative emotions that you are currently experiencing. From your list, choose one negative emotion that you struggle the most with. Using a recipe format, write down your own recipe to overcome sadness, anger, jealousy, loneliness, confusion, etc. Think of all of the "ingredients" that help you when you are feeling that way. Share your recipe with others in the group.

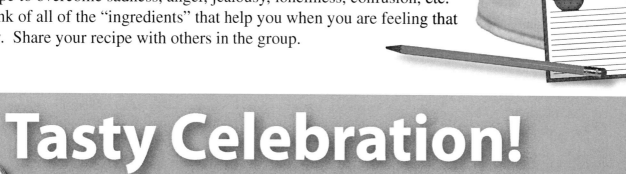

Tasty Celebration!

Directions: What was your special person's favorite food? In celebration of their life, prepare that recipe and bring it to share with the group. Make copies of the recipe with your name and the name of your special person for everyone in the group. Enjoy!

Comfort Jar

Objective: For group members to identify their support systems and strengths.

Materials Needed:
- One clean, empty peanut butter jar per person
- Puff paint
- Strips of colored paper
- Pens/pencils

Directions:

Have group members decorate their jars with puff paint in memory of the person who died.

On the strips of paper, write down things that bring you comfort. It may be a happy memory of the person who died, an activity you enjoy doing, a person that you can talk to, or a strength that you have. Write down all of these on the strips of paper and place them in your jar.

Keep your jar in a special place. When you are feeling sad or having a bad day, pull out one of your strips and read it to remind yourself of the supports and strengths you have in your life.

My Should'a, Could'a, Would'a Moment

Objective: To recognize the painful moments we are still holding on to, and to begin to let go of some of our guilt.

Materials needed:
- Small strips of paper
- Balloons
- String or ribbon
- Helium

We all have things that we wish we had done/said/ acted differently. However we cannot dwell on those things and we cannot live in the past.

Directions:

1. Take some time to think about your "should'a, could'a, would'as." (i.e. I should have stayed home that evening and not gone out. I wish I could have said "I love you" one last time.)

2. Write each of your "should'a, could'a, would'as" down on a separate piece of paper.

3. Reflect on each should'a, could'a, would'a, and pick one that you are ready to let go of.

4. Roll or fold that piece of paper and place it inside of the balloon.

5. Inflate the balloon with helium, tie it off and attach a ribbon or string to it.

6. As a group, go outside to release the balloons. As you let go of your string, release some of the guilt and regret that you are holding onto. Say goodbye to your "Should'a, Could'a, Would'as" and let it go…forever!

(Group members can keep their remaining "should'a could'a woulda's" and release them when they feel they are ready to do so.

Piecing It All Together

Materials Needed:
100 piece puzzle
Markers

Directions:

1. At the end of each session, pass out a puzzle piece (or 2-3 pieces) to each group member (including yourself.) Pass out enough pieces each time so that all of the pieces will be decorated by the last grief session.

2. Have group members decorate the back of the puzzle piece and/or write down something that they found helpful in the session.

3. During the last session, have the group put the puzzle together on a cookie sheet using the original picture side (not the side that they have decorated.)

4. Place a cutting board on top of the completed puzzle and flip it over so that all of the group's work is showing.

5. Discuss the unique qualities and strengths that everyone brought to the group to create the whole. "Through the support of one another, we have come a little further on our grief journey."

6. Celebrate all that you have accomplished.

You may choose to coat the puzzle with glue and let it harden so that it can be displayed as a whole.

My Petrified Memory

Objective: Preserve your favorite memory of the person who died.

Materials Needed:
Pieces of freshly cut wood
Clear wood finish or sealer
Glue
Paper
Crayons, Markers, Pens, Pencils etc.

Directions: Think of your favorite memory with the person who died. Draw a small picture of your memory, or type/write it out on paper. Glue the paper to the piece of wood. Seal the paper onto the wood with wood sealer and let dry. Now your favorite memory will be preserved in your mind and on your special piece of petrified wood forever.

Blessing Chain

Objective: To identify the ways in which the person who died was a blessing in the group member's life.

Materials Needed:
- Colored Paper
- Scissors
- Pens or markers
- Glue sticks

Directions:

Have each child cut strips of colored paper. On each strip, have them write one way in which the person who died was a blessing. Maybe it was something nice they did for the group member or others. Maybe it was something the group member learned from that person. Or maybe it is a special memory. What did that person leave behind?

Have each group member make a paper chain out of their strips. Discuss how even though this person is no longer physically present, the things they did and taught remain with us. By remembering these things and using the things they taught us, they can continue to live on in our hearts.

Hang the chain in your room to remind you of all of the ways your special person was a blessing in your life.

Memory Book

A Memory Book
in Honor of

_____

Write name on line

Place a photo of your loved one above and place the
obituary of your loved one on the inside of the cover.

This is a picture of my family before

_____ died.

This is a picture of my family now.

Here is a picture of what grief looks like to me.

_____'s favorite holiday was _____

_____ because:

_____

_____

_____

_____

Draw a picture of you and _____
celebrating his/her favorite holiday.

_____'s Favorites:

Food:

Movie:

TV Show:

Dessert:

Color:

Hobby:

Draw a picture of _____ doing his/her favorite thing.

This is what I remember about your funeral or memorial service:

_____

_____

_____

_____

Draw a picture of the funeral or memorial service:

A Special Memorial

If I could design a special headstone or urn for you,
this is what it would look like:

Write a letter to the person who died.
What would you say to that person if he or she were here right now?
What would you want that person to know?

Dear _____,

_____

_____

_____

_____

_____

_____

_____

_____

_____

_____

_____

Your special person has read the letter that you wrote. What would that person want to say in a letter written back to you? Write a letter from him/her to you. What would he/she want you to know?

Dear _____,

_____

_____

_____

_____

_____

_____

_____

_____

_____

_____

_____

_____

_____

This is what I miss most about _____.
(draw a picture and label it)

If _____ was still here, this is what I would want to do with him/her: (draw a picture and label it)

I will never forget you

_____.

You will live inside of my heart **forever**.

My best memory of

_____

_____

_____

_____

_____

_____

_____